M & M

and

The Mummy Mess

By Pat Ross · Pictures by Marylin Hafner

PUFFIN BOOKS

PUFFIN BOOKS

A Division of Penguin Books USA Inc.
375 Hudson Street, New York, New York 10014
Penguin Books Ltd, 27 Wrights Lane, London W8 5TZ England
Penguin Books Australia Ltd., Ringwood, Victoria, Australia
Penguin Books Canada Ltd, 2801 John Street, Markham, Ontario, Canada L3R 1B4
Penguin Books (N.Z.) Ltd, 182–190 Wairau Road, Auckland 10, New Zealand

Penguin Books Ltd, Registered Offices: Harmondsworth, Middlesex, England
First published by Viking Penguin Inc. 1985
Published in Puffin Books 1986
5 7 9 8 6 4
Text copyright © Pat Ross, 1985
Illustrations copyright © Marylin Hafner, 1985
All rights reserved

Printed in U.S.A.

Set in Times Roman

Library of Congress Cataloging in Publication Data
Ross, Pat.   M&M and the mummy mess.
Summary: Best friends Mandy and Mimi have a scary time when their eagerness to
see mummies leads them to sneak into the new museum exhibit a week before it opens.
[1. Mummies—Fiction.   2. Museums—Fiction]   I. Hafner, Marylin, ill.   II. Title.
PZ7.R71973Maam   1986   [E]   85-73264   ISBN 0-14-032084-9

For my friend, John Laufer

Chapter One

It was Saturday morning.

Mandy and Mimi,
the friends M and M, were going to the
natural history museum together.

They knew this museum very well.
When they were babies, their mothers
brought them there in strollers.

"Remember how we used to think
the giant whales would get us?"
said Mandy.

"Babies aren't so smart,"
sighed Mimi.

The friends M and M still went to
the museum, but now they went
without their mothers.

They still visited the whales.

They never missed the dinosaurs.

And they always quacked at the
stuffed birds. But not this time.

This time they were going for
the new show that opened
at noon.

M and M wanted to be the first
in line for Mummy Wonders.

They'd read a lot about mummies.
But they had never seen one.

When they passed a water fountain,
Mandy and Mimi stopped for a drink.

"Promise you won't laugh if
I tell you a secret?" said Mandy.

"I promise," said Mimi, who
liked secrets.

"Well," Mandy whispered, "sometimes I think mummies are too creepy. And maybe they're just pretending to be dead."

Mimi started to laugh. Then she remembered her promise.

"These mummies have been dead for thousands of years," Mimi told Mandy.

"What about that mummy movie we saw on TV?" said Mandy. "First the mummies broke open their cases. Then they turned people like us into mummies."

"I *loved* that movie!" cried Mimi. "*Escape of the Doomed Mummies*. It was so disgusting.

But it was only a movie."

"I sure hope so," said Mandy.
"I like mummies, but not enough
to be one."

The museum was filled with people.
Mandy and Mimi looked for a
sign about the new mummy show.
But the only sign in the lobby said:

"We've seen that," said Mandy.

"Five times," groaned Mimi.

Mandy checked the news clipping.
It told all about the mummy show.

"It's in the East Hall," she told
Mimi. So they headed for the East Hall.

On the way, the friends passed
the stuffed birds without quacking.

They ran right past the dinosaur
room without looking.

"Slow down," said Mandy.
"There's nobody ahead of us."
And it was true that the hallway
leading to Mummy Wonders was empty.

The closer they got to the East Hall,
the darker it got.

When they rounded the corner,
they knew something was wrong.

The East Hall was very quiet.
There was a rope across the doorway,
and a sign that said:

PEOPLE
WORKING

Mandy and Mimi had been
waiting all week. How could
Mummy Wonders be closed?

Mandy read the news story again.

"Oh, no," she said, showing
the story to Mimi. "I was so
excited, I got the date wrong."

"The big day is *next* Saturday,"
said Mimi sadly, reading over
Mandy's shoulder.

Mandy stuffed the clipping
in her pocket and started to go.

"Wait!" cried Mimi.
"I'll bet they wouldn't mind
if we had a sneak preview.
You know, that's when certain people
get in ahead of everybody else."

Mandy and Mimi looked beyond the
ropes. They could see wooden cases.

And they were sure they could
see real mummies at the back
of the room.

"Museums like kids to be
curious," said Mandy.

So the friends ducked under
the rope and went into the hall of
Mummy Wonders alone.

Chapter Two

"It's dark," said Mandy.

"That's just to get you in the mood," said Mimi.

"It sure is working," said Mandy.

"Hey," Mimi went on cheerfully, "What did the child say to its mummy?"

"Okay, what?" asked Mandy, feeling better now.

"Unwrap me. I'm dying in here!" cried Mimi, who loved mummy jokes.

M and M's laughter echoed
in the big, dark room.

The two friends made their way
to the back of the room.
They were sure the real mummies
were there.

They passed one long, wooden
mummy case after another.

Then, all of a sudden, M and M
saw three strange bodies standing
against the wall. And they
were not mummies.

"They're *dummies,*" said Mandy.
"Like the ones you see undressed
in store windows. I wonder what
they're doing here."
Then they saw a sign that said:

SPECIAL EXHIBIT
How a
Mummy
is Wrapped

Next to the sign was a big roll of
cloth, very much like the cloth that
real mummies are wrapped in.

"I've got it," said Mimi. "They're going to wrap the dummies to make mummies. Let's check this out."

So Mandy and Mimi stopped and looked at the wrapping cloth.

"It looks like bandages," said Mimi. "Let's see how it works. Stand still."

So Mandy stood still,
with her arms out to the sides.
And Mimi started to wrap.

Mimi wrapped Mandy's arms.
She finished the first one quickly.

"Hey, this is fun!" said Mandy.

"This is hard work," said Mimi.

She wrapped the second arm,
then all five fingers on each hand.

"I wonder why they wrapped
them," said Mimi, still working hard.

"I've got a book that tells all
about it," said Mandy.
It was to keep their bodies
from rotting and falling apart."

"Yuck," said Mimi, going on
to Mandy's body.

Mandy could feel the cloth
getting tighter and tighter.

"It's like a giant cast," said
Mandy, who was wondering if being
wrapped was really so much fun.

Mimi finished the body and went on to the legs.

"Why would anyone care so much about a yucky dead body?" Mimi wondered out loud.

"Well," said Mandy, glad she knew more than Mimi, "the ancient Egyptians were sure they went someplace else after they died."

"I get it!" cried Mimi, wrapping faster and tighter now. "And they wanted to make sure their bodies were ready for the trip."

"They even took their special
things along," said Mandy,
who felt an itch start on her elbow.

"I'd take my bottle cap
collection," said Mimi.

"You couldn't even be a mummy,"
said Mandy.

"How come?" Mimi was finishing
the legs now.

"Because only kings and queens
and very important people could
be mummies," Mandy explained.

"Well, maybe I would have been a princess. Then I'd get to take my bottle cap collection. You don't know," added Mimi.

"I do know—" began Mandy.

"*I* know," broke in Mimi, "that you sound like a mummy book somebody ought to shut!"

She laughed at her own joke.

"And besides," Mimi added, stepping back, "you're finished. I did a great job. You'll last a thousand years, at least."

"Maybe you did too good a job," said Mandy. "I can't bend my legs."

"Something's not quite right," said Mimi.

"I'm glad you noticed," said
Mandy, feeling the itch start up again.

"I forgot the head."

"Not my face!" cried Mandy.

Soon, Mandy was wrapped from head to toe.

Just then, Mandy and Mimi heard voices in the hall. And the voices were headed their way.

"Oh, no! It's the people who work on the mummies," cried Mandy.

Chapter Three

The voices got closer and closer.

"Don't move," whispered Mimi.

"I can't," whispered Mandy,
trying to move her stiff mummy legs.

Then Mimi hid behind a dummy.

And Mandy stood like a mummy.

The workers walked right past mummy Mandy, who wondered if museum people really wanted children to be *that* curious.

The workers walked past Mimi, who was hiding behind a dummy. And Mimi wondered if sneak previews were a good idea after all.

Then, all of a sudden, somebody patted mummy Mandy on the back. It was a tall man in a white coat. His name tag said DIRECTOR.

This is it! thought Mandy.

We've had it! thought Mimi.

"Who wrapped the short one?" asked the director.

No one answered.

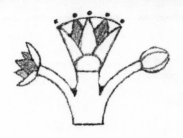

Then, from behind a dummy,
came a funny little voice.
"I did," it said.

"Nice work," said the director,
looking at mummy Mandy.
"It looks so real."

And then he walked away.

Quietly, Mimi tiptoed over.

"Shhh," she whispered.
And she unwrapped Mandy's legs.

Then, as fast as they could,
Mandy and Mimi ducked under the
rope.

Chapter Four

Mimi headed for the doorway.
Mandy followed. The loose cloth
flapped around her legs as she ran.

"Hey, you two!" someone shouted.

"We should stop," puffed Mandy.

"Let's find a ladies' room first,"
said Mimi. "Then we can talk about
who read the date wrong and got us
into this mummy mess."

She looked hard at Mandy.

"We did it *together!*" said Mandy.
"A mummy mess for both of us!"

"Okay," agreed Mimi, pointing
to a narrow door with no sign.
"In here! Quick!"

It was dark inside. And it
smelled funny. It smelled like
the science corner at school when the
experiment went wrong.

"They don't keep the bathrooms
very nice here," said Mimi.

She searched for the light switch.
The room was dark. But over
by a window, M and M could see
a strange shape. It was hanging
from the ceiling, upside-down.

The shape did not look like
anything that belonged in a bathroom.
It looked like a huge bird that
belonged in a zoo—behind bars.

Mimi found a row of switches.
She turned them all on at once.

Now the room was filled with light.
Mandy and Mimi could see
the huge bird by the window,
and hundreds of its strange friends—
on shelves, in cases, and hanging, too.

"They're stuffed!" cried Mandy
in relief.

"Like the birds we always quack
at," cried Mimi. "This must be
the room where they work on the
birds for the museum. Wait till
we tell our science class
about this!"

"Wait till we tell our science class
we got put in jail," said Mandy.

Suddenly Mimi looked worried.
"We have to give ourselves up,"
she said. "And now."

Then Mimi took Mandy's hand.
And without a word, the friends
turned off the lights and left the
bird room together.

They were headed back down the
hall when they heard someone
shout, "Stop that mummy!"

"Hey! You two!" cried a voice they
knew from before.

Chapter Five

And there was the man in the
white coat with a name tag
that said DIRECTOR.

What the man saw was a
mummy and a mummy's friend,
looking very upset.
There was just no way to hide
the mummy mess they were in.

The director took one look
and he started to say something.

"We didn't mean—" broke in
Mandy.

"My goodness," the director
cried out. "A mummy who talks!"

And he began to smile a little.

"We were just curious," said Mimi.

"Well, you do nice work,"
said the director, looking at Mimi's
wrapping job. "But you're
a week early!"

Then he looked serious and tapped
his foot on the floor.

Suddenly it was very quiet.

Mandy and Mimi were afraid
to say another word.

Then, "Didn't you see the signs?"
the director asked more firmly.

Mandy and Mimi nodded their
heads "Yes."

"And didn't you see the rope?"
M and M were really worried now.

They hoped he hadn't seen
them leave the rare bird room, too.

"And the bird room is no
hiding place," he said.

M and M had been in messes
before, but this was the worst.

"I think I know just the thing
to keep two curious girls out of
trouble," he said, more kindly.

Mimi began to unwrap Mandy.

"Don't unwrap your friend,"
said the director. "I have a plan."

Mandy was sure the director
would leave her wrapped forever.

Mimi was sure the director
would never let her come back.

"Follow me," said the director.

They passed the whales and
the dinosaurs and the stuffed birds.

At last they came to the lobby.

There the director handed Mimi
a stack of fliers to hand out.
The fliers said:

COMING SOON

MUMMY
WONDERS
THE MUSEUM OF NATURAL HISTORY

"We're really sorry," M and M said.
And they meant it.

"I know," said the director.

"But you gave me a great idea."

Then he made a sign and hung
it on Mandy.

The sign said:

"You two should be the best kind
of advertising for Mummy Wonders,"
he said.

So Mandy and Mimi
gave out fliers. And they talked
about wrapping mummies to the
children.

M and M did such a good job that
the director invited them back.

The very next Saturday,
Mandy and Mimi came at noon.
They looked in on the whales.
They waved at the dinosaurs.
They quacked at stuffed birds.

And they took their places
at the front of the line to see
Mummy Wonders—without any
mummy mess, this time.